THE MUMMY CODE

Level 4H

Written by Melanie Hamm
Illustrated by Roger Simó
Reading Consultant: Betty Franchi

About Phonics

Spoken English uses more than 40 speech sounds. Each sound is called a *phoneme*. Some phonemes relate to a single letter (d-o-g) and others to combinations of letters (sh-ar-p). When a phoneme is written down, it is called a *grapheme*. Teaching these sounds, matching them to their written form, and sounding out words for reading is the basis of phonics.

Early phonics instruction gives children the tools to sound out, blend, and say the words without having to rely on memory or guesswork. This instruction gives children the confidence and ability to read unfamiliar words, helping them progress toward independent reading.

About the Consultant

Betty Franchi is an American educator with a Bachelor's Degree in Elementary and Middle Education as well as a Master's Degree in Special Education. Betty holds a National Boards for Professional Teaching Standards certification. Throughout her 24 years as a teacher, she has studied and developed an expertise in Phonetic Awareness and has implemented phonetic strategies, teaching many young children to read, including students with special needs.

Reading tips

This book focuses on the ō sound (made with the letter formation *o–e*) as in h**o**m**e**.

Tricky and/or new words in this book

Any words in bold may have unusual spellings or are new and have not yet been introduced.

> **Tricky and/or new words in this book**
>
> **mystery golden strange knew there symbols saw would stretched treasure half awesome voice**

Extra ways to have fun with this book

After the readers have read the story, ask them questions about what they have just read.

What did Ambrose discover in the tunnel?
What was your favorite part of the story?

This must be a secret code. What does it mean?

A Pronunciation Guide

This grid contains the sounds used in the stories in levels 4, 5, and 6 and a guide on how to say them.

/ă/ as in pat	/ā/ as in pay	/âr/ as in care	/ä/ as in father
/b/ as in bib	/ch/ as in church	/d/ as in deed/ milled	/ĕ/ as in pet
/ē/ as in bee	/f/ as in fife/ phase/ rough	/g/ as in gag	/h/ as in hat
/hw/ as in which	/ĭ/ as in pit	/ī/ as in pie/ by	/îr/ as in pier
/j/ as in judge	/k/ as in kick/ cat/ pique	/l/ as in lid/ needle (nēd'l)	/m/ as in mom
/n/ as in no/ sudden (sŭd'n)	/ng/ as in thing	/ŏ/ as in pot	/ō/ as in toe
/ô/ as in caught/ paw/ for/ horrid/ hoarse	/oi/ as in noise	/o͝o/ as in took	/ū/ as in cute

/ou/ as in out	/p/ as in pop	/r/ as in roar	/s/ as in sauce
/sh/ as in ship/ dish	/t/ as in tight/ stopped	/th/ as in thin	/th/ as in this
/ŭ/ as in cut	/ûr/ as in urge/ term/ firm/ word/ heard	/v/ as in valve	/w/ as in with
/y/ as in yes	/z/ as in zebra/ xylem	/zh/ as in vision/ pleasure/ garage/	/ə/ as in about/ item/ edible/ gallop/ circus
/ər/ as in butter			

Be careful not to add an /uh/ sound to /s/, /t/, /p/, /c/, /h/, /r/, /m/, /d/, /g/, /l/, /f/ and /b/. For example, say /fff/ not /fuh/ and /sss/ not /suh/.

Ambrose Jones had a nose
for **mystery**. When he dug
up a **golden** box with a

strange note inside, he **knew**
he must decode it.

"**There** is a mole. A mole digs.
Those trees are in a grove.
I need to dig in a grove,"
Ambrose speculated.

He rode until he found a grove.
It was a brilliant stroke of luck.

Ambrose dug a hole until he found
a tunnel. The tunnel sloped both

ways. Ambrose chose the left slope
and hoped he was right.

On the stone wall there
were more **symbols**, a robe,
and a throne.

"Hmm," Ambrose pondered,
"whose home is this?"

"Mine," came a muffled tone.
Ambrose froze.

He was not alone.

In an alcove he **saw** a casket.
Ambrose crept close.

The **voice** spoke. "You woke me.
Now let me out!"

Ambrose was choked with fear.
He broke the seal and lifted the lid.

Would he see bones? No!
A mummy rose from the casket.

The mummy **stretched** and strode around. "I have dozed too long. My bones are stiff," the mummy joked.

"Now, Ambrose Jones, can you crack this one last code?" The mummy pointed to a coin and a crown.

"A **treasure** trove!" cried
Ambrose Jones. "Come and
look," the mummy proposed.

"Long ago I was king of **half** the globe." Ambrose Jones had a nose for mystery. "**Awesome**!" he said.

OVER 48 TITLES IN SIX LEVELS
Betty Franchi recommends...

Other titles to enjoy from Level 4

The Circus Mice	Monster's Night	Jemima The Spy
978 1 84898 783 8	978 1 84898 784 5	978 1 84898 785 2

Some titles from Level 5

The Gigantic Bear	Celebrity Celia	The Cemetery Dance
978 1 84898 787 6	978 1 84898 788 3	978 1 84898 789 0

Some titles from Level 6

Hugh is New	Clumsy Eagle	Bad Zombie Movie
978 1 84898 791 3	978 1 84898 792 0	978 1 84898 793 7

An Hachette Company
First published in the United States by TickTock, an imprint of Octopus Publishing Group.
www.octopusbooksusa.com

Copyright © Octopus Publishing Group Ltd 2013

Distributed in the US by
Hachette Book Group USA
237 Park Avenue, New York NY 10017, USA

Distributed in Canada by
Canadian Manda Group
165 Dufferin Street, Toronto, Ontario, Canada M6K 3H6

ISBN 978 1 84898 786 9

Printed and bound in China
10 9 8 7 6 5 4 3 2 1